HARPERFESTIVAL IS AN IMPRINT OF HARPERCOLLINS PUBLISHERS.

MAN OF STEEL: SUPERMAN SAVES SMALLVILLE
COPYRIGHT © 2013 DC COMICS.
SUPERMAN AND ALL RELATED CHARACTERS AND ELEMENTS ARE TRADEMARKS OF AND © DC COMICS.
(s13)

HARP29970

FOR INFORMATION ADDRESS HARPERCOLLINS CHILDREN'S BOOKS, A DIVISION OF HARPERCOLLINS PUBLISHERS,
10 EAST 53RD STREET, NEW YORK, NY 10022.
WWW.HARPERCOLLINSCHILDRENS.COM

LIBRARY OF CONGRESS CATALOG CARD NUMBER: 2012955958
ISBN 978-0-06-223603-6

BOOK DESIGN BY JOHN SAZAKLIS

13 14 15 16 17 CWM 10 9 8 7 6 5 4 3 2 1
❖
FIRST EDITION

SUPERMAN
SAVES SMALLVILLE

MAN OF STEEL™

ADAPTED BY JOHN SAZAKLIS
ILLUSTRATED BY JEREMY ROBERTS

INSPIRED BY THE FILM MAN OF STEEL
SCREENPLAY BY DAVID S. GOYER
STORY BY DAVID S. GOYER AND CHRISTOPHER NOLAN

SUPERMAN CREATED BY JERRY SIEGEL AND JOE SHUSTER

HARPER FESTIVAL
An Imprint of HarperCollinsPublishers

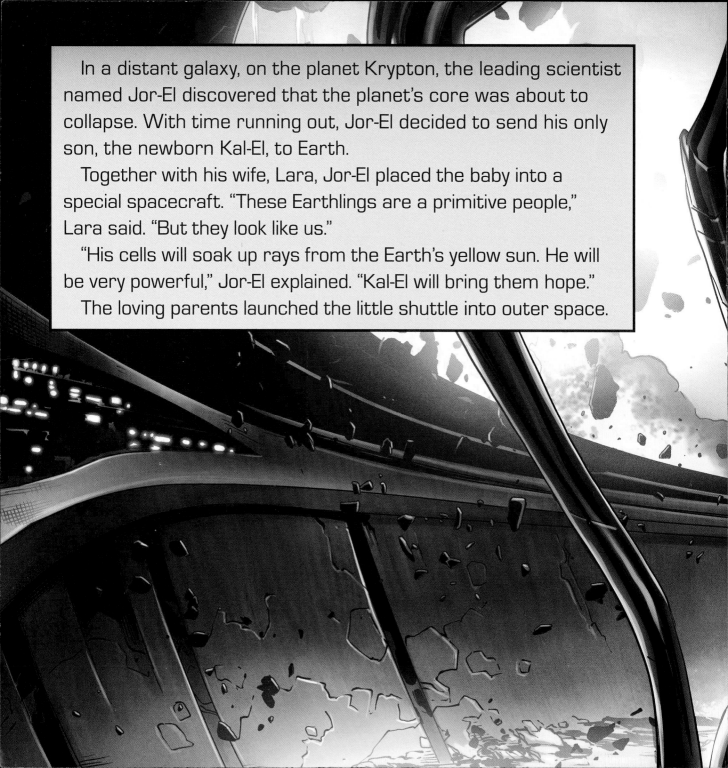

In a distant galaxy, on the planet Krypton, the leading scientist named Jor-El discovered that the planet's core was about to collapse. With time running out, Jor-El decided to send his only son, the newborn Kal-El, to Earth.

Together with his wife, Lara, Jor-El placed the baby into a special spacecraft. "These Earthlings are a primitive people," Lara said. "But they look like us."

"His cells will soak up rays from the Earth's yellow sun. He will be very powerful," Jor-El explained. "Kal-El will bring them hope."

The loving parents launched the little shuttle into outer space.

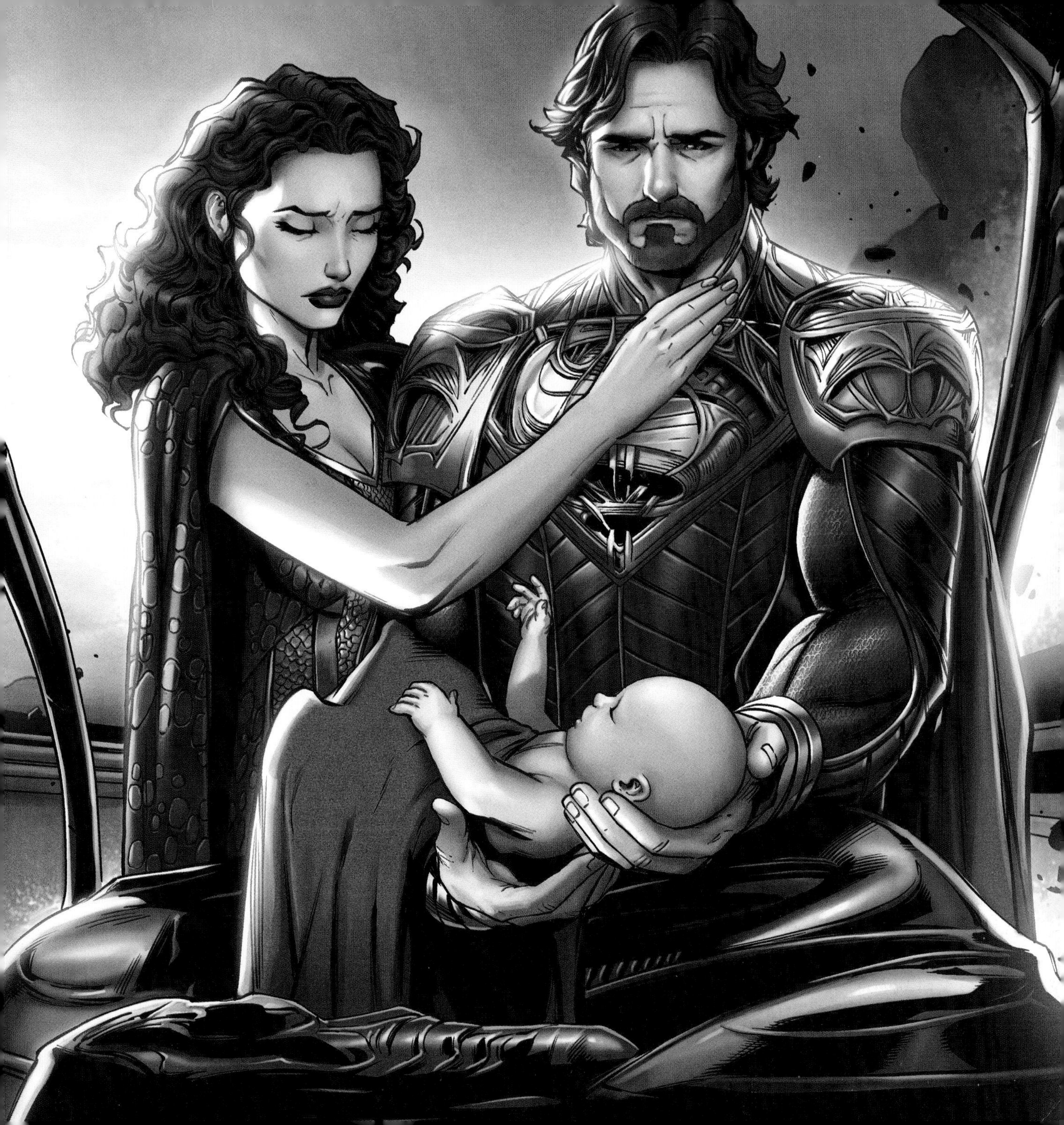

After Kal-El's parents said good-bye to him and watched his ship zoom off toward his new home, the ground began to shake. The walls began to crumble around them. They were sad they could not save their planet, but they knew that Kal-El would be safe.

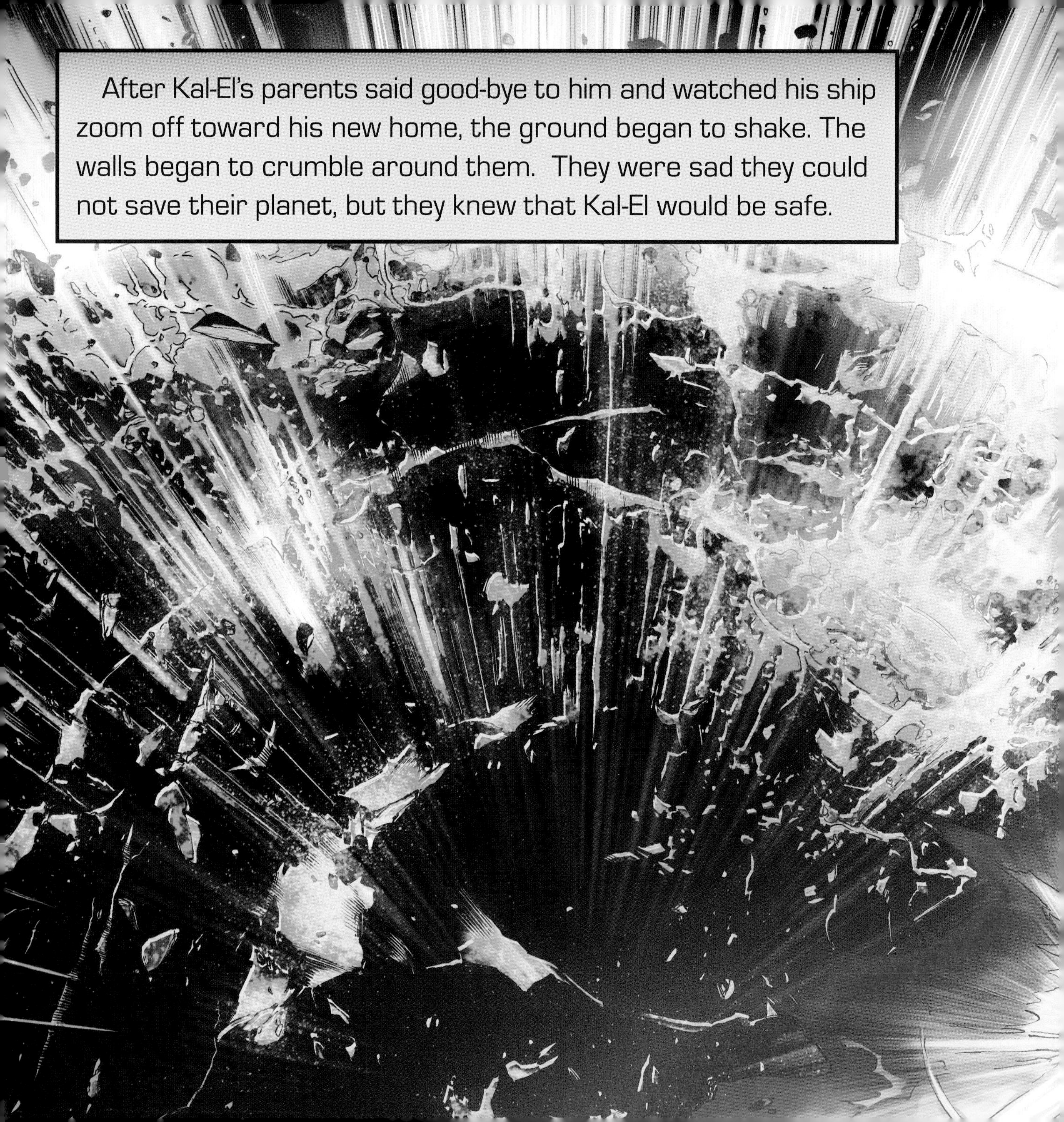

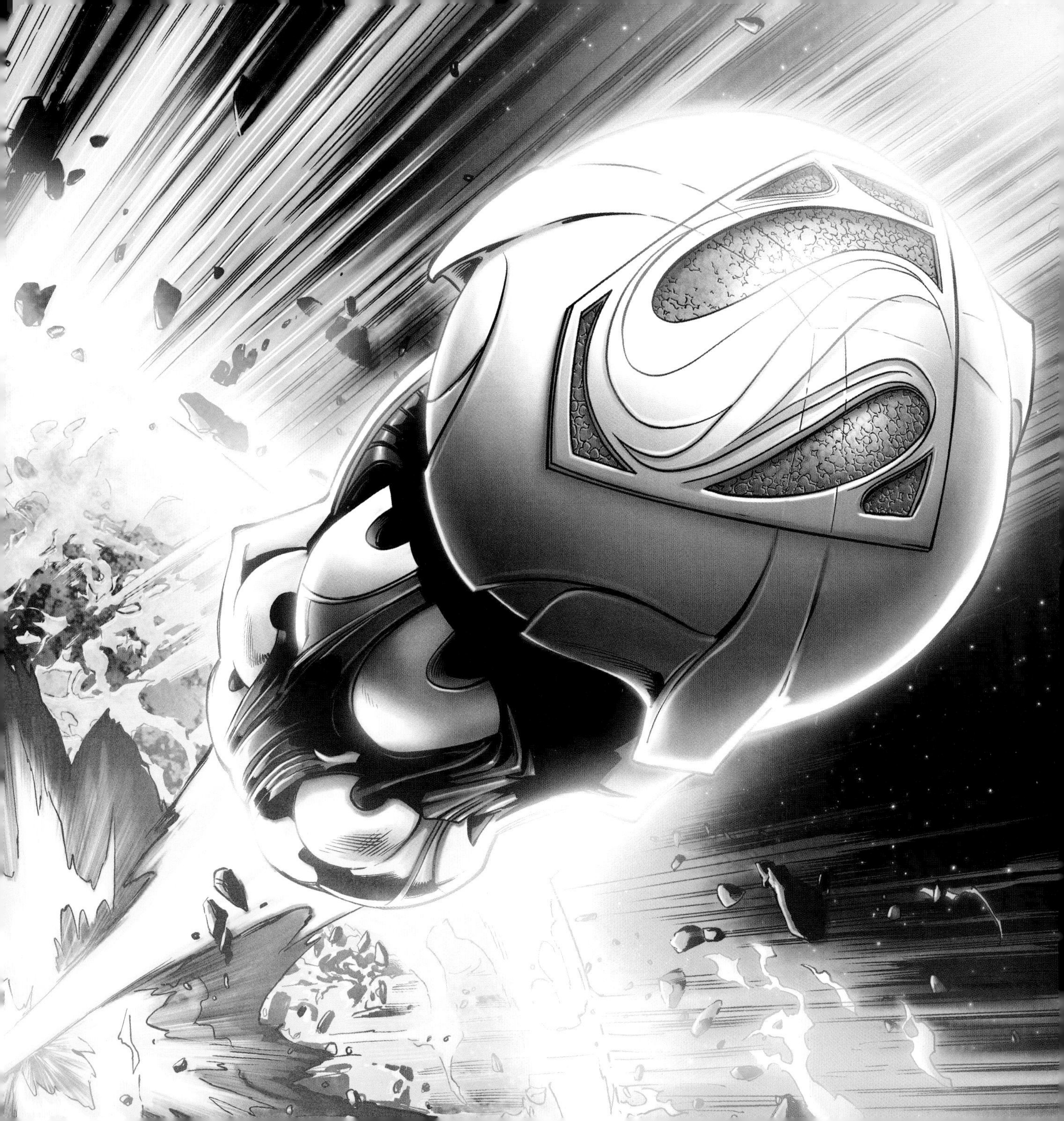

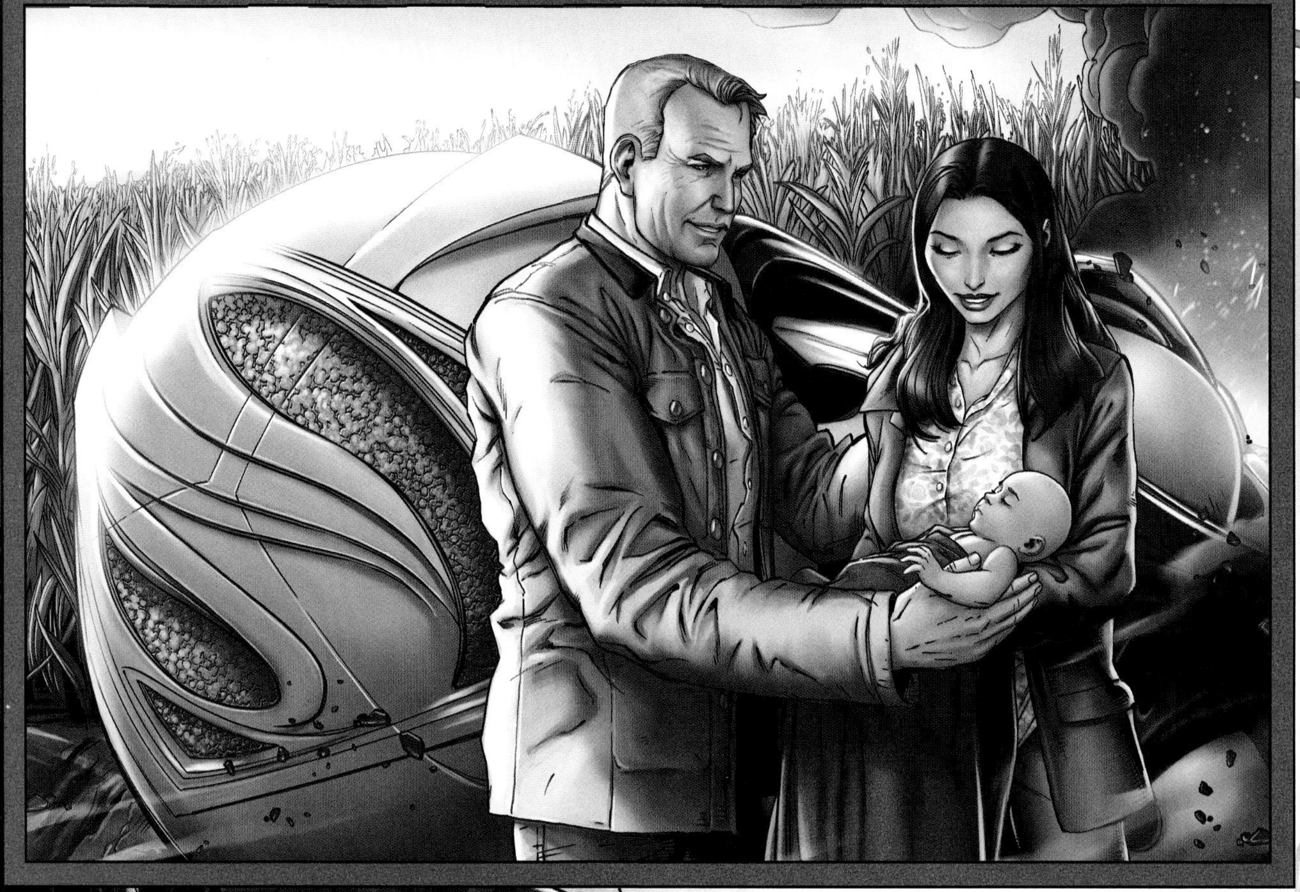

Kal-El's spacecraft zoomed through Earth's atmosphere, crash-landing on a cornfield in Smallville, Kansas.

Young farmers Jonathan and Martha Kent discovered the shuttle. They adopted the baby and raised him as their own, naming him Clark.

Clark's alien cells adapted to his new environment as he grew older. The process was slow and painful, but he developed a number of special abilities.

Aside from his incredible strength and speed, Clark had amazing senses, such as X-ray vision, super-hearing, and heat vision. He could fly, too!

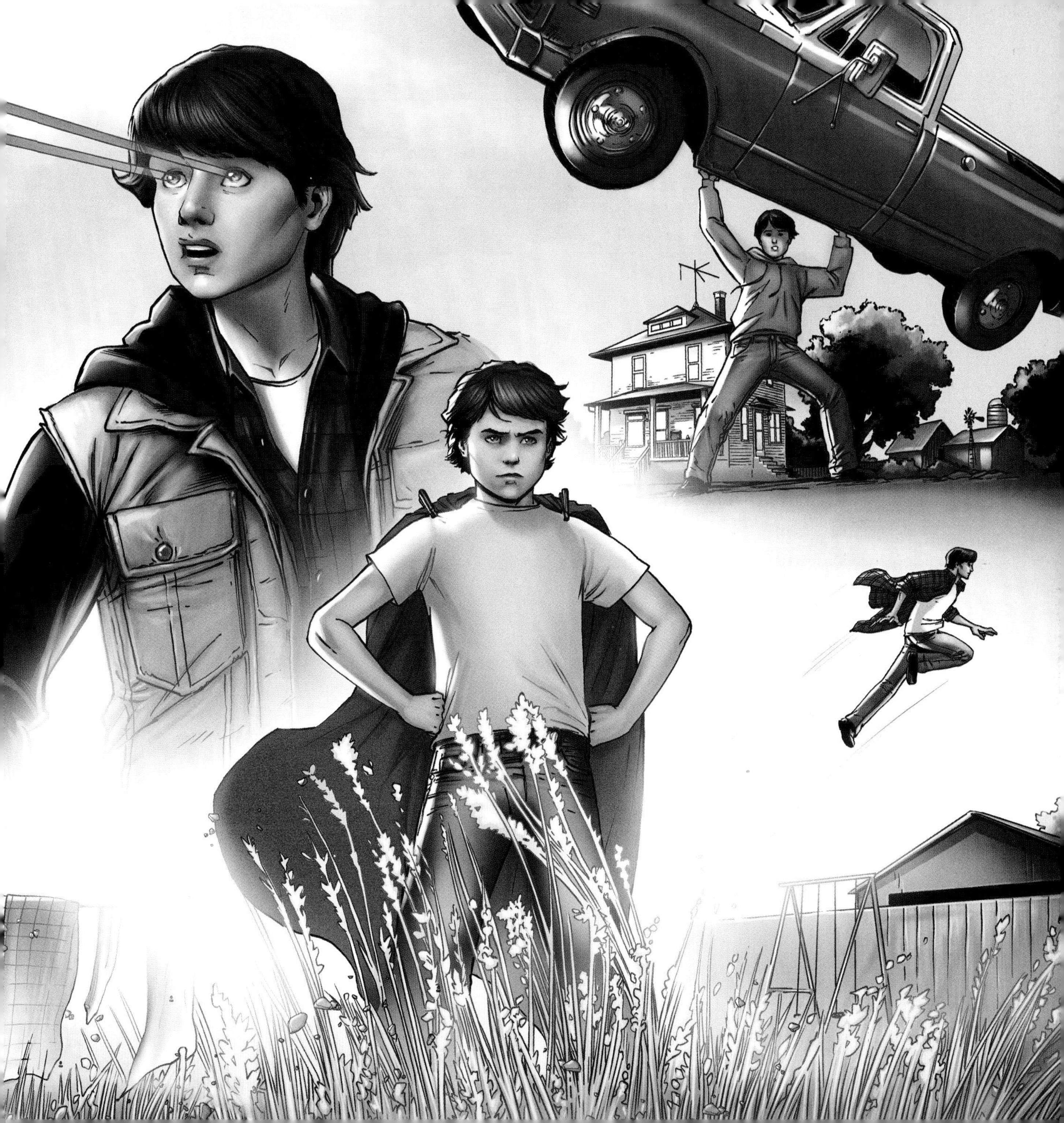

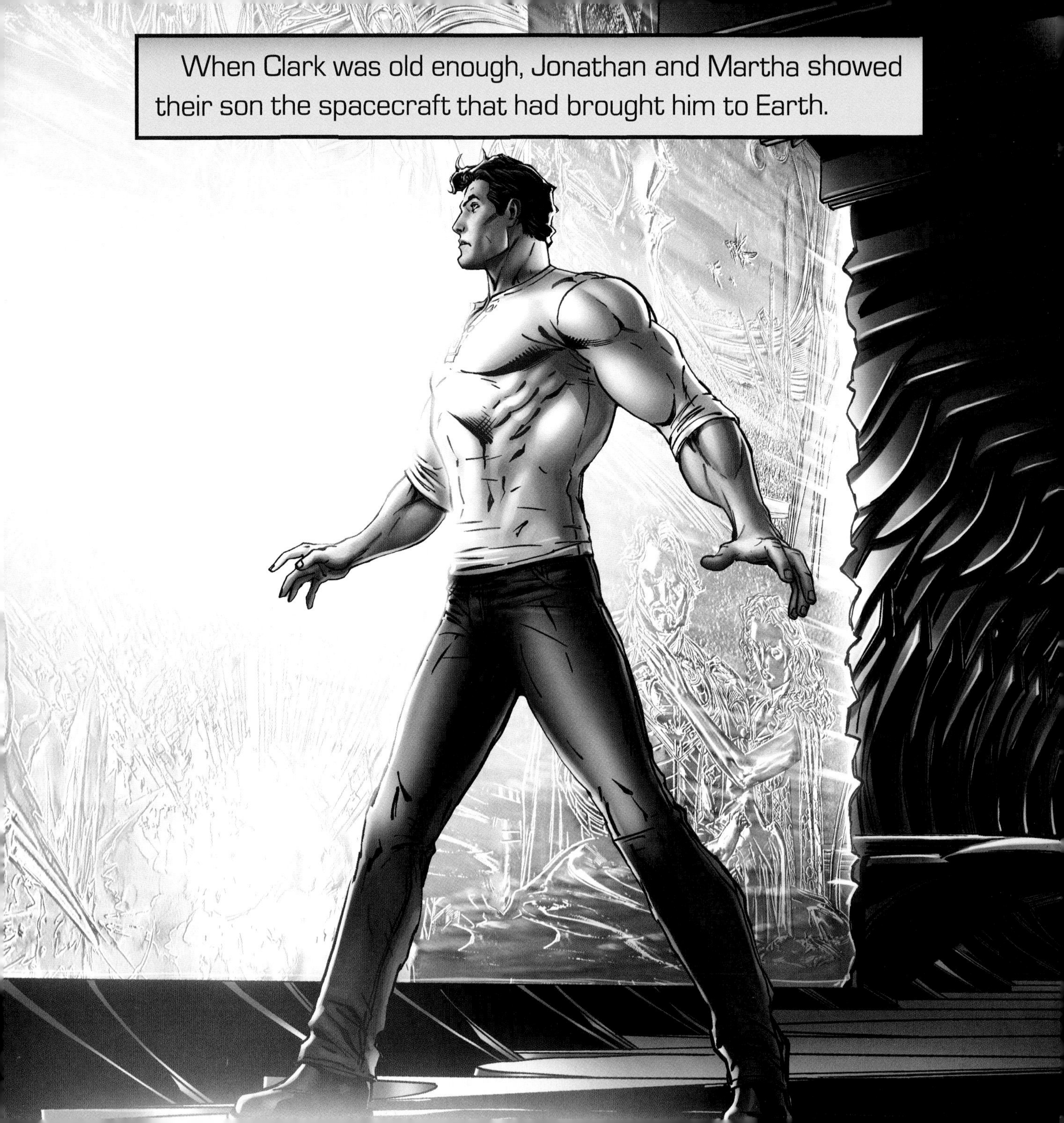
When Clark was old enough, Jonathan and Martha showed their son the spacecraft that had brought him to Earth.

The shuttle contained information on the doomed planet of Krypton. Clark learned about his real parents, Jor-El and Lara, and that his name was really Kal-El. He also learned about General Zod, Faora, and Nam-Ek, three of the most dangerous criminals in Krypton's history.

Kal-El vowed to fulfill his parents' dream and bring hope to the people of Earth.

He became the hero known as Superman!

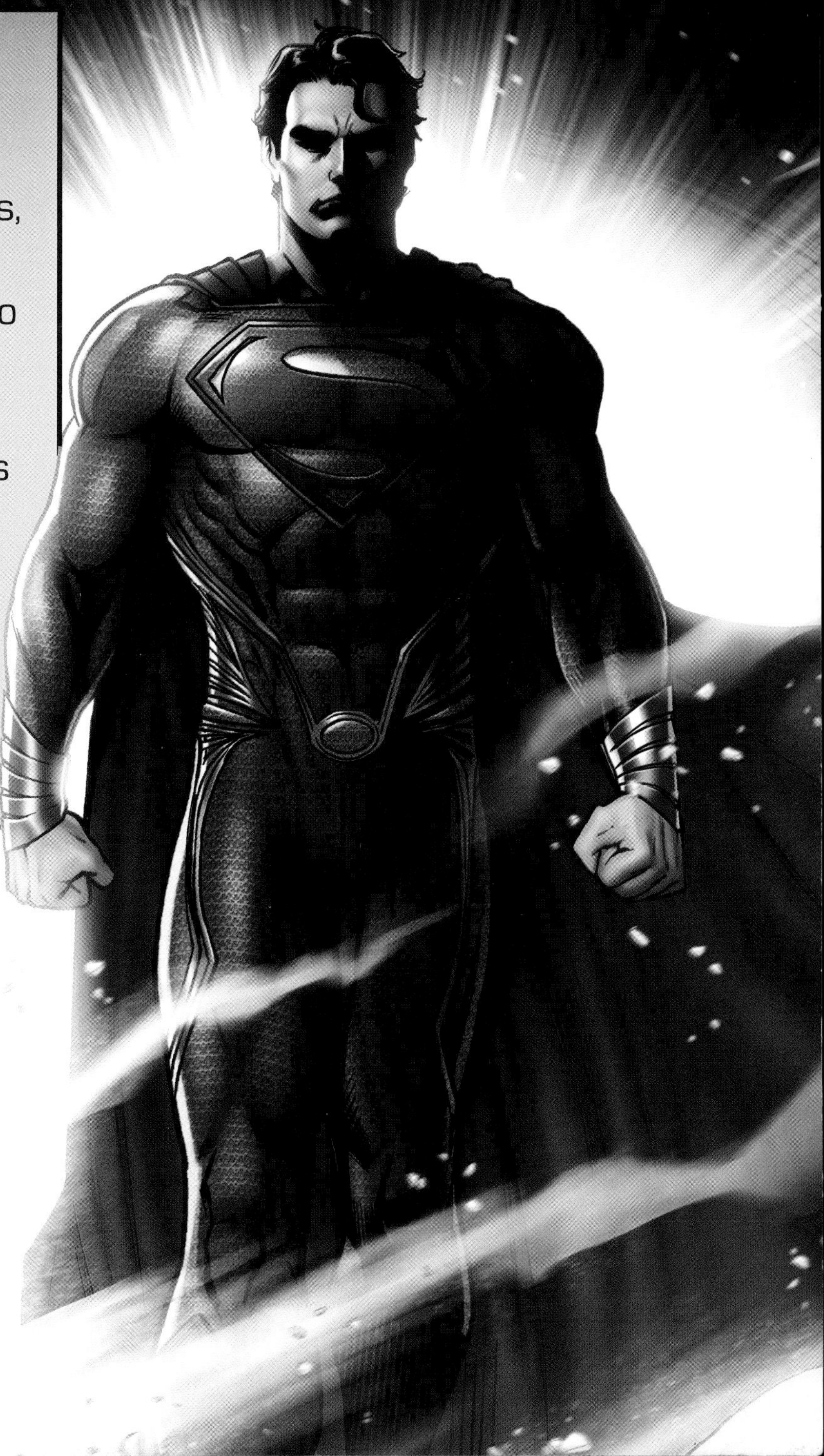

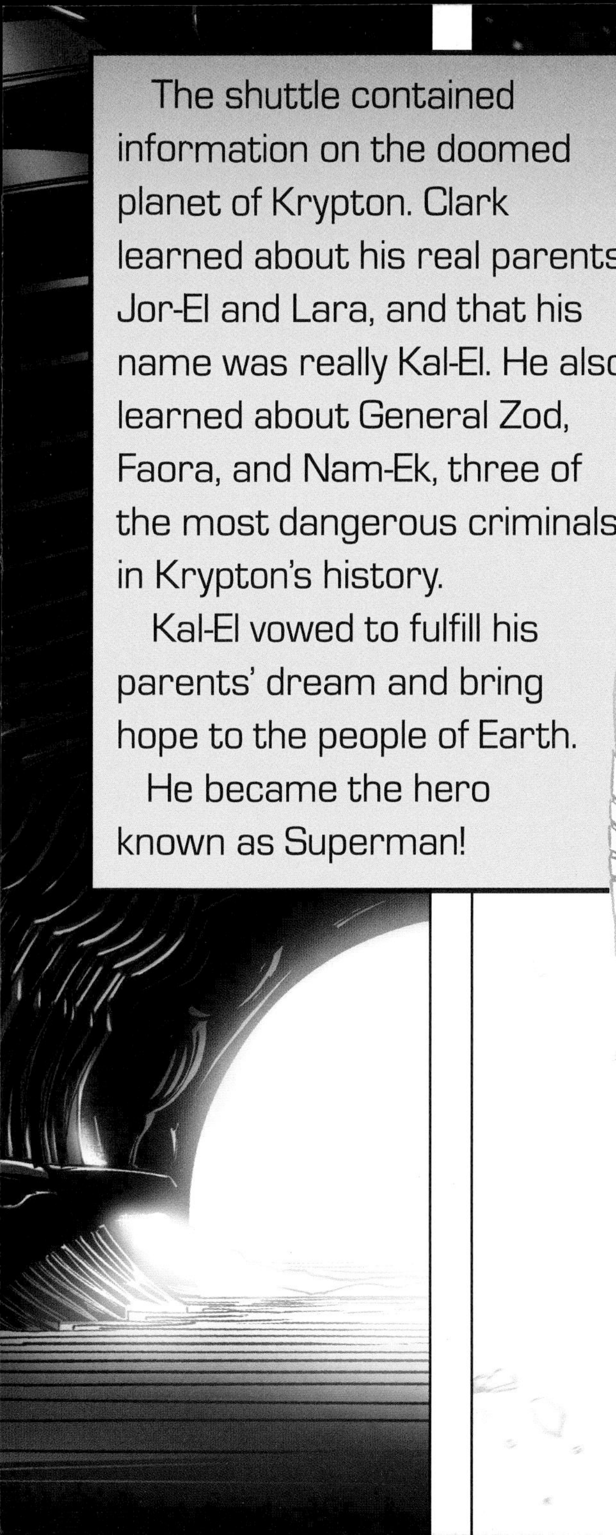

Clark did not know it, but the three Kryptonian criminals he learned about were on the loose!

"Let us go to Earth," Faora said to General Zod.

The general agreed. "Earth will be a very suitable planet for us."

They navigated their spaceship toward the blue and green planet. When they entered the Earth's atmosphere, they soared above the United States.

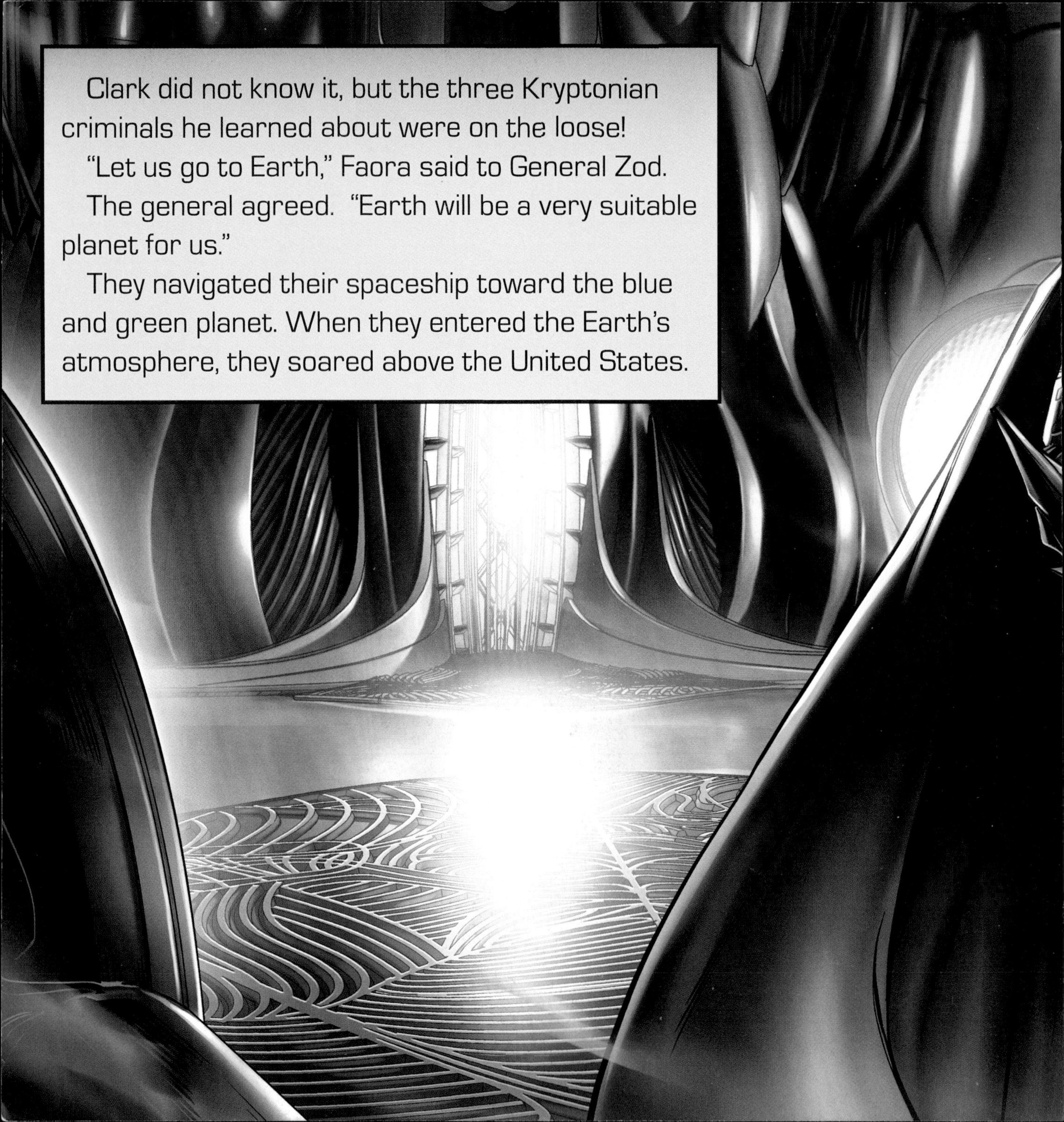

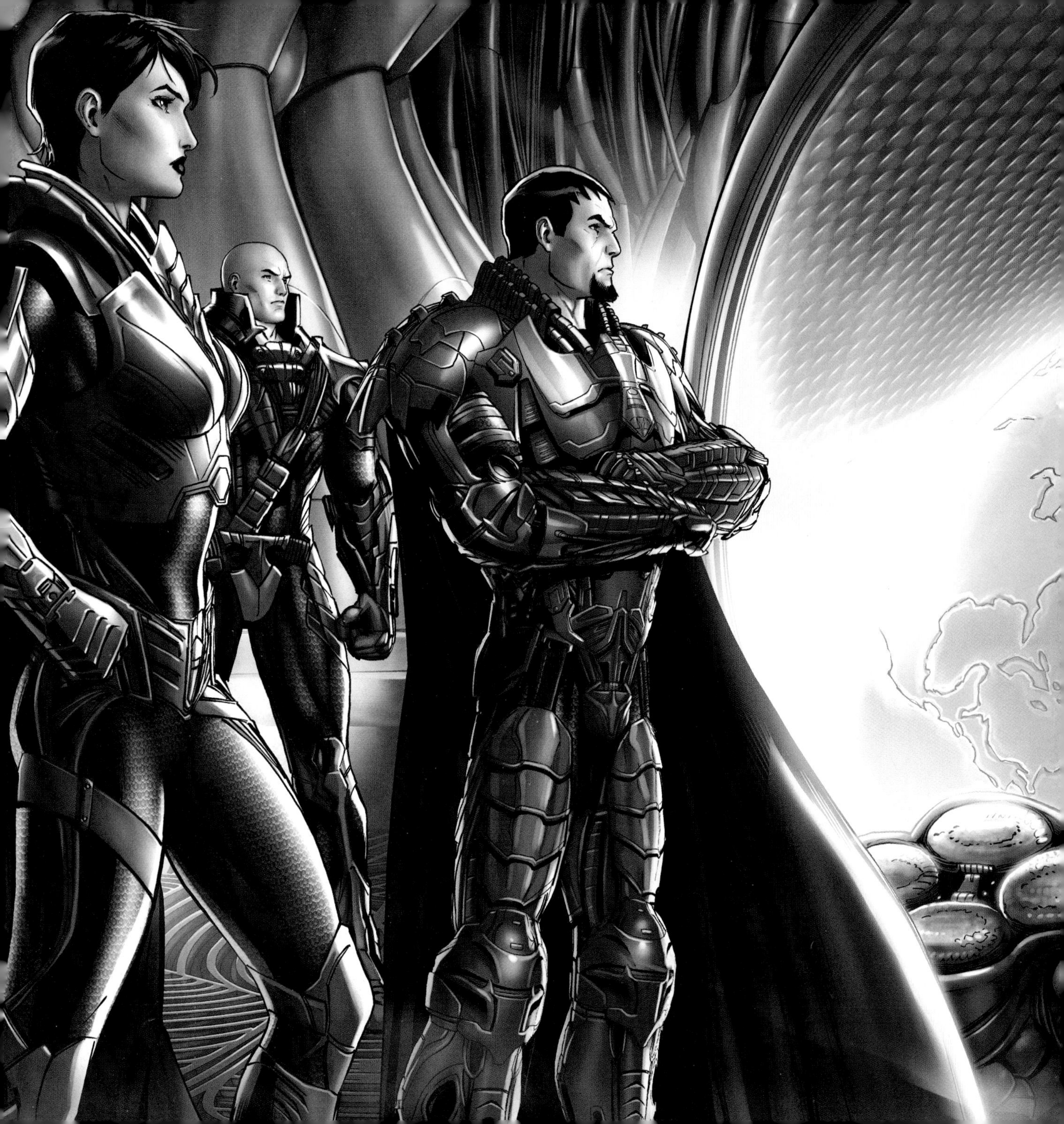

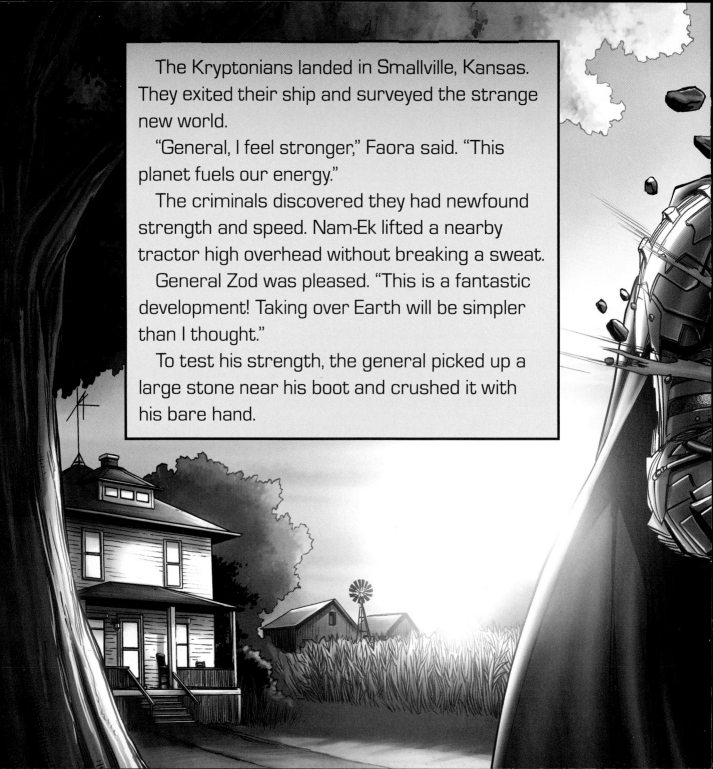

The Kryptonians landed in Smallville, Kansas. They exited their ship and surveyed the strange new world.

"General, I feel stronger," Faora said. "This planet fuels our energy."

The criminals discovered they had newfound strength and speed. Nam-Ek lifted a nearby tractor high overhead without breaking a sweat.

General Zod was pleased. "This is a fantastic development! Taking over Earth will be simpler than I thought."

To test his strength, the general picked up a large stone near his boot and crushed it with his bare hand.

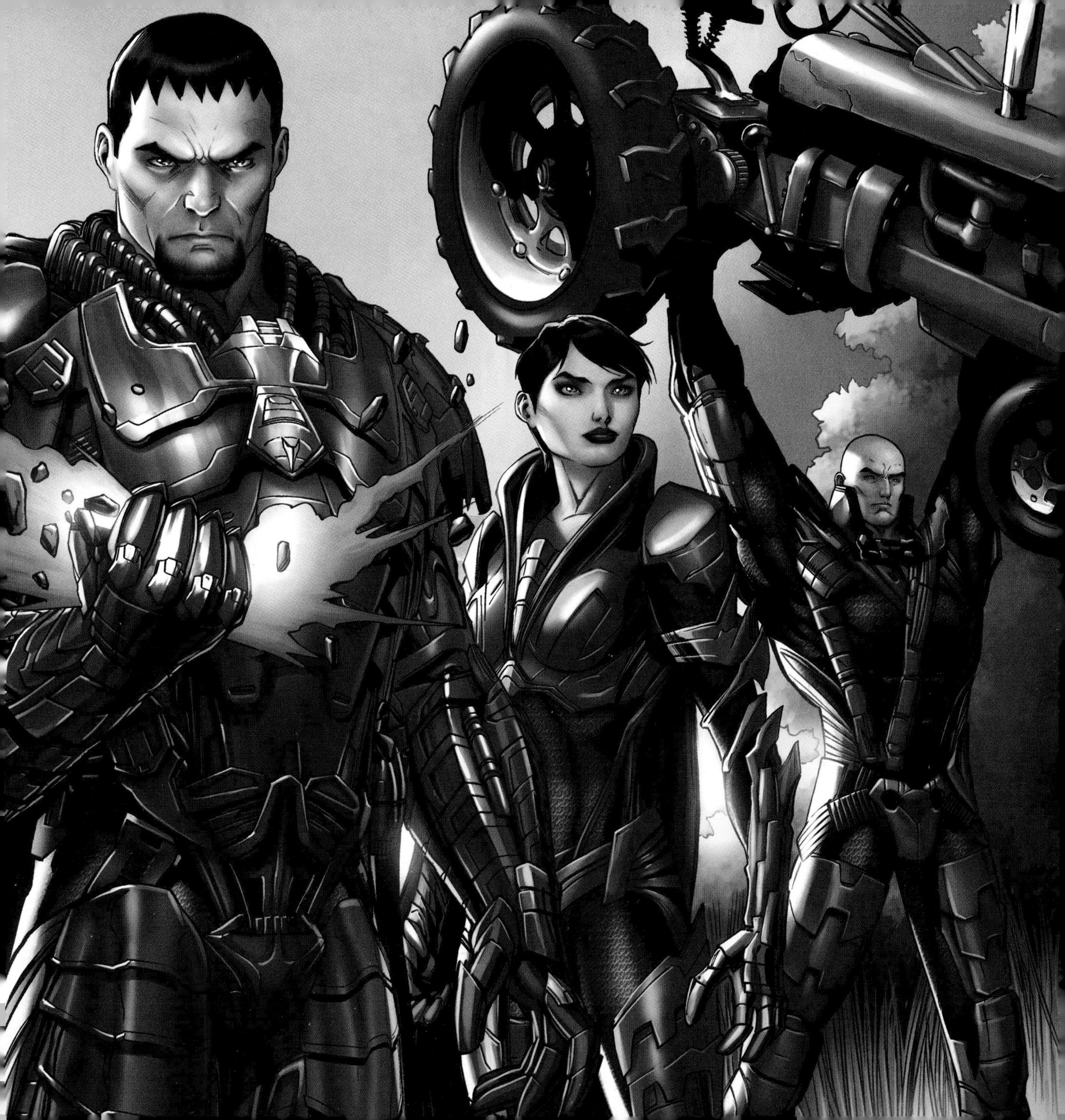

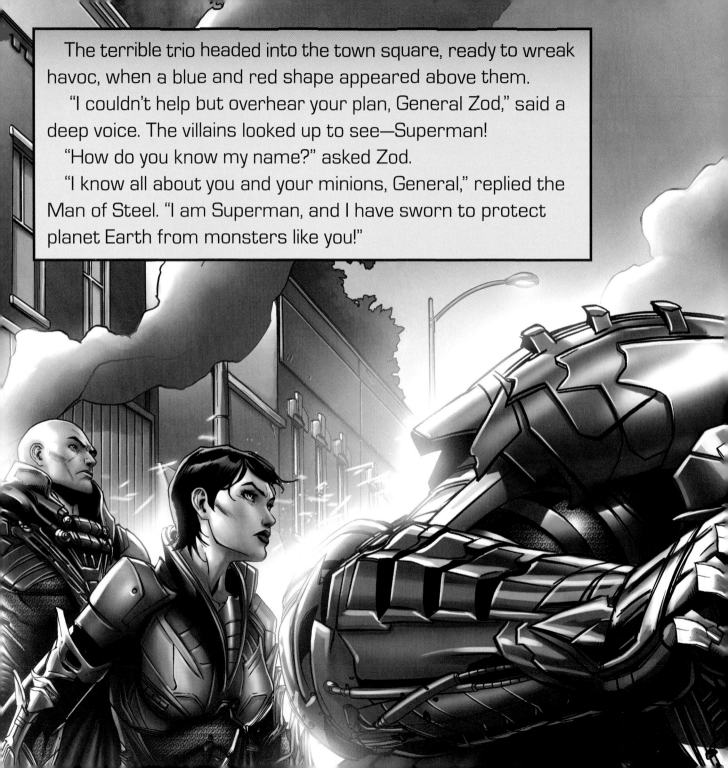

The terrible trio headed into the town square, ready to wreak havoc, when a blue and red shape appeared above them.

"I couldn't help but overhear your plan, General Zod," said a deep voice. The villains looked up to see—Superman!

"How do you know my name?" asked Zod.

"I know all about you and your minions, General," replied the Man of Steel. "I am Superman, and I have sworn to protect planet Earth from monsters like you!"

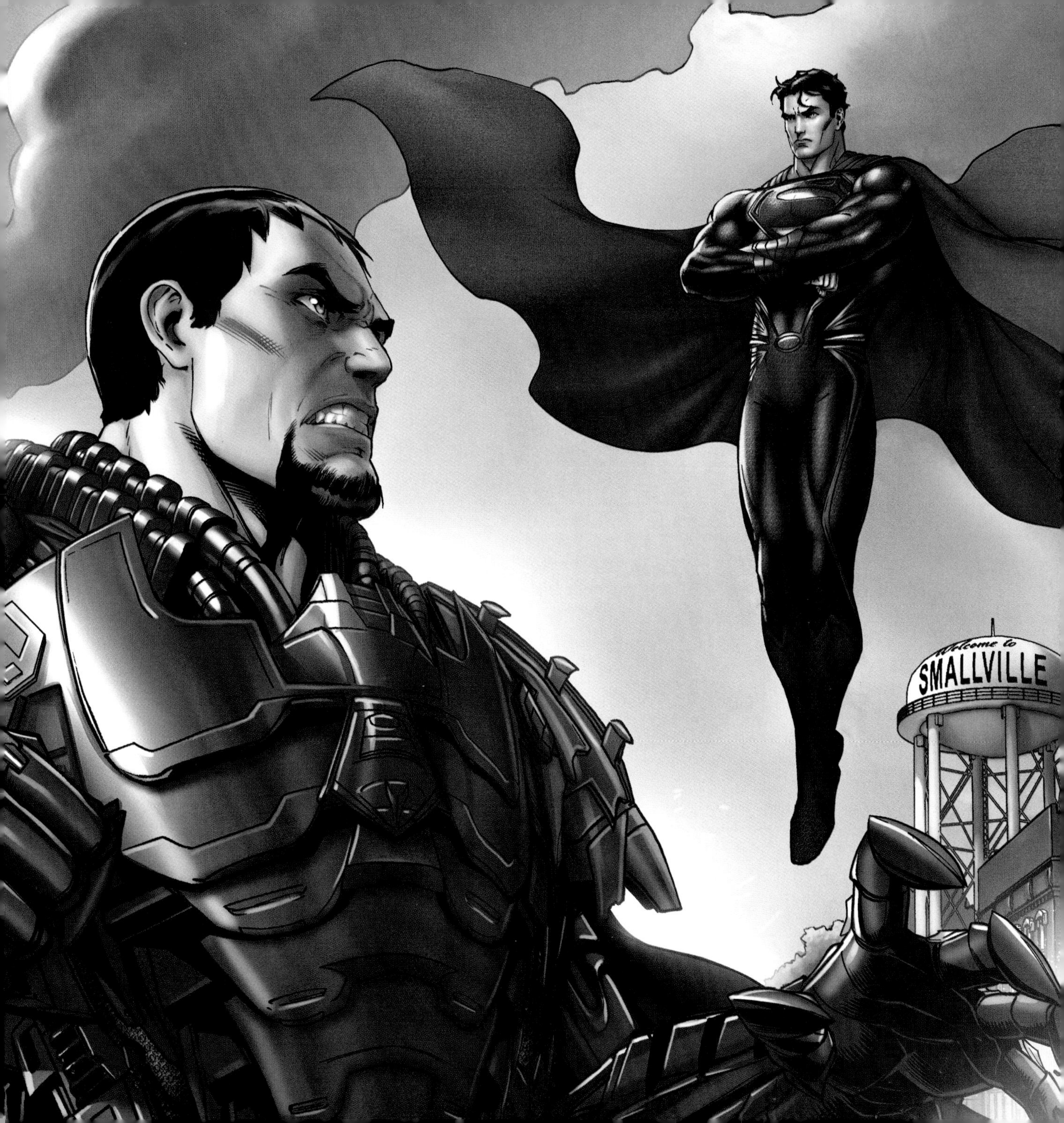
Welcome to
SMALLVILLE

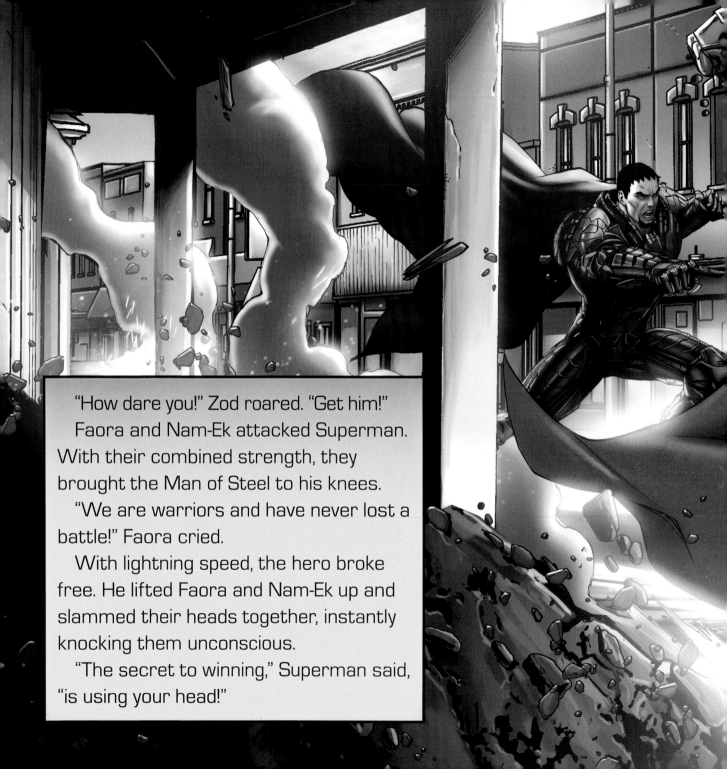

"How dare you!" Zod roared. "Get him!"

Faora and Nam-Ek attacked Superman. With their combined strength, they brought the Man of Steel to his knees.

"We are warriors and have never lost a battle!" Faora cried.

With lightning speed, the hero broke free. He lifted Faora and Nam-Ek up and slammed their heads together, instantly knocking them unconscious.

"The secret to winning," Superman said, "is using your head!"

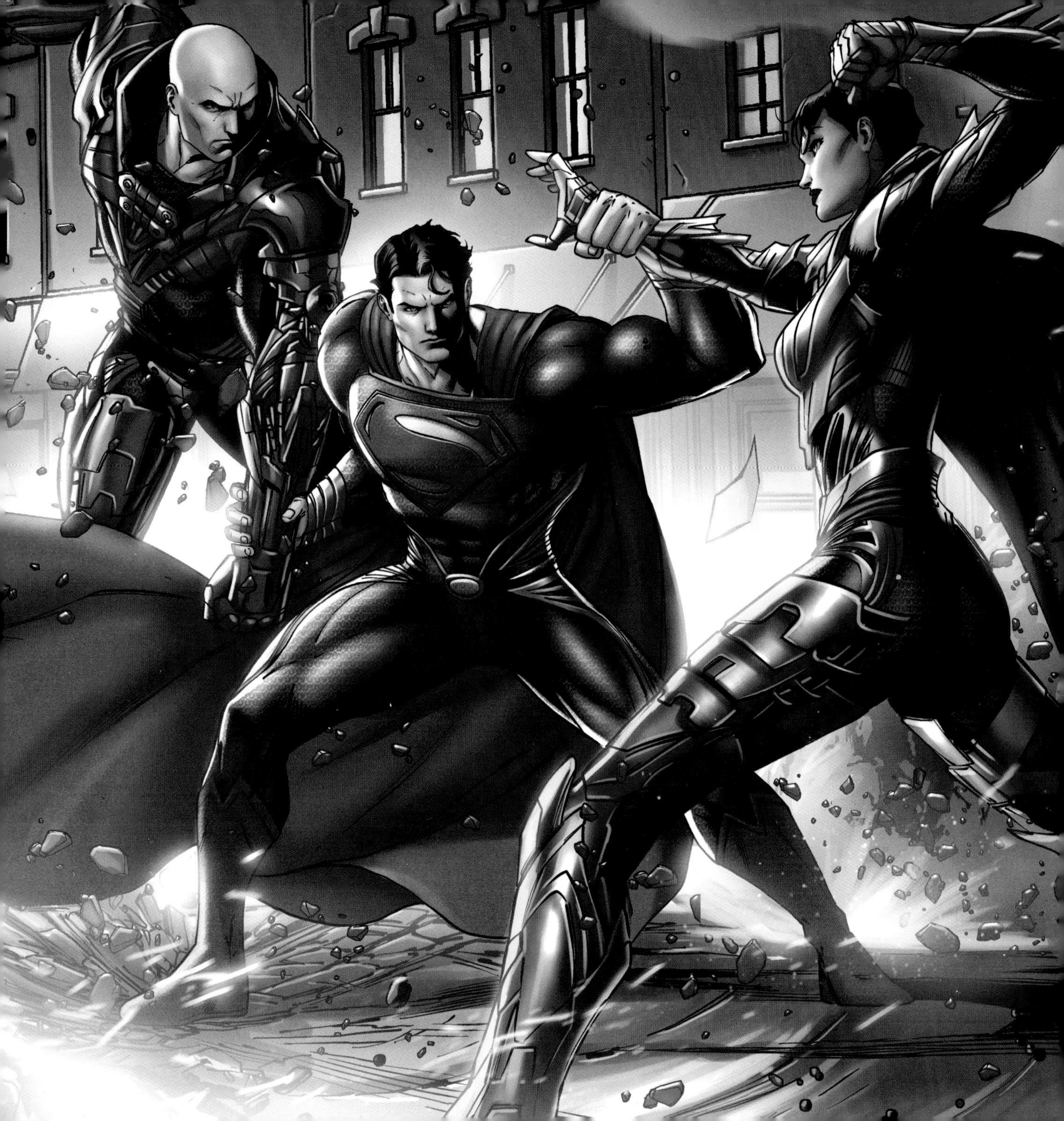

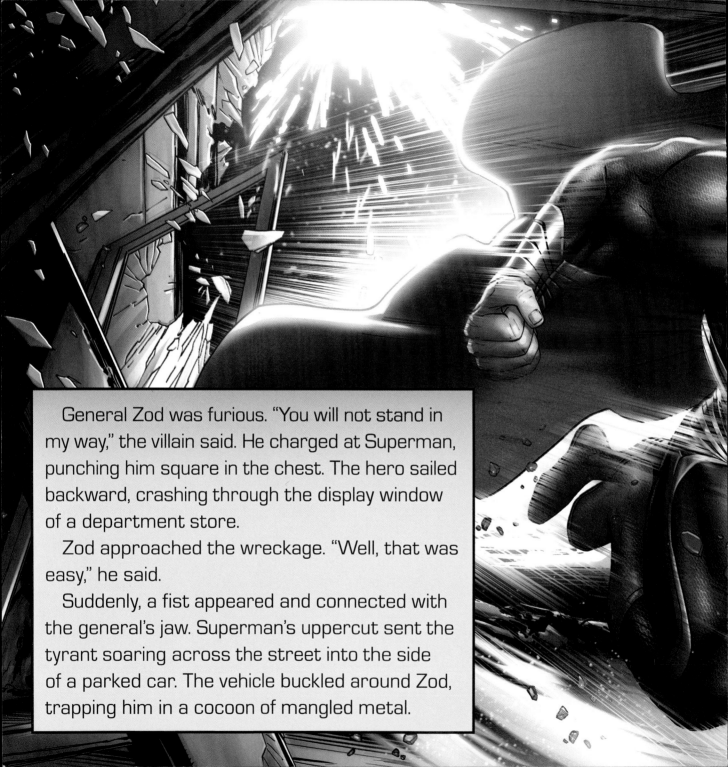

General Zod was furious. "You will not stand in my way," the villain said. He charged at Superman, punching him square in the chest. The hero sailed backward, crashing through the display window of a department store.

Zod approached the wreckage. "Well, that was easy," he said.

Suddenly, a fist appeared and connected with the general's jaw. Superman's uppercut sent the tyrant soaring across the street into the side of a parked car. The vehicle buckled around Zod, trapping him in a cocoon of mangled metal.

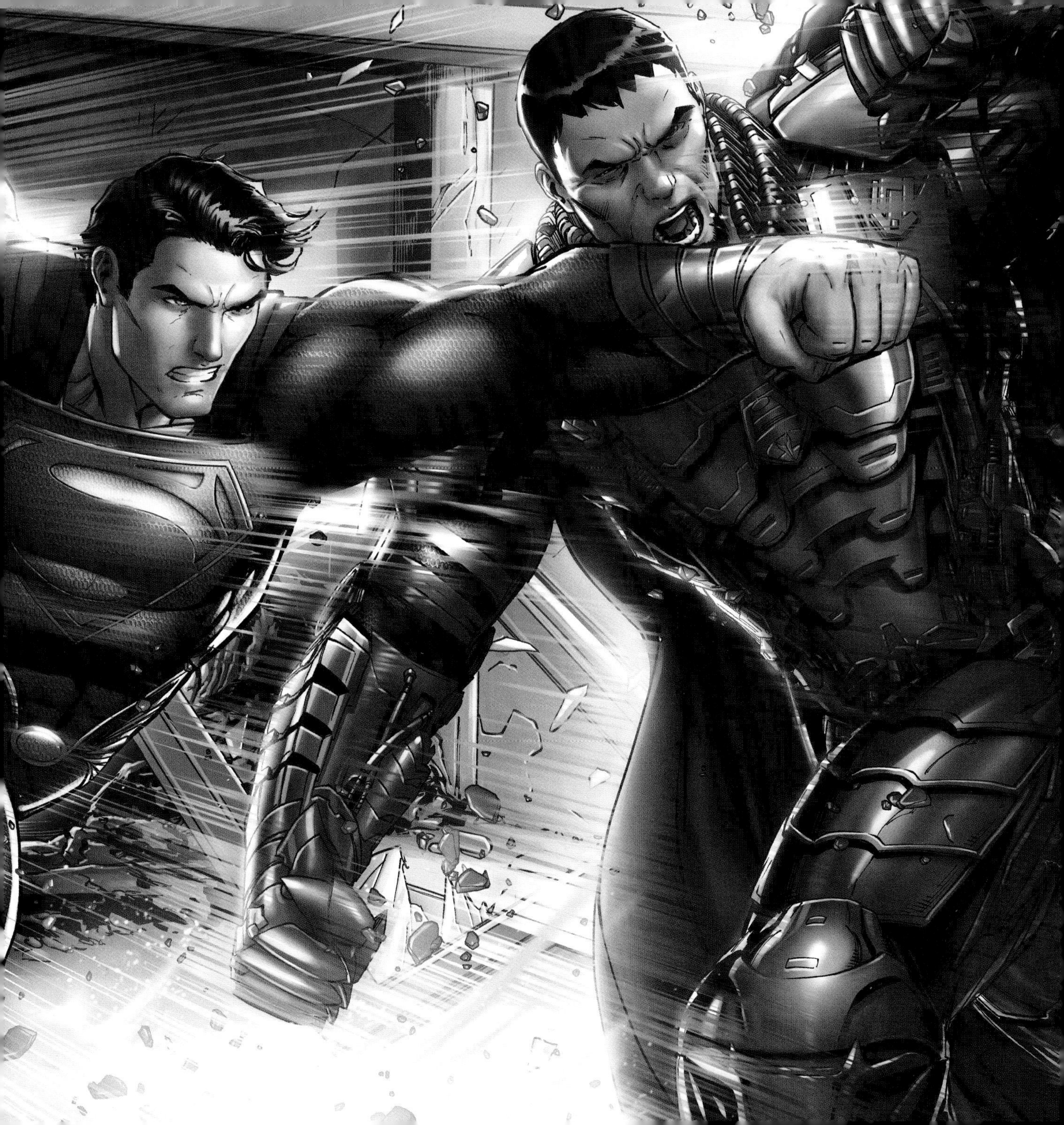

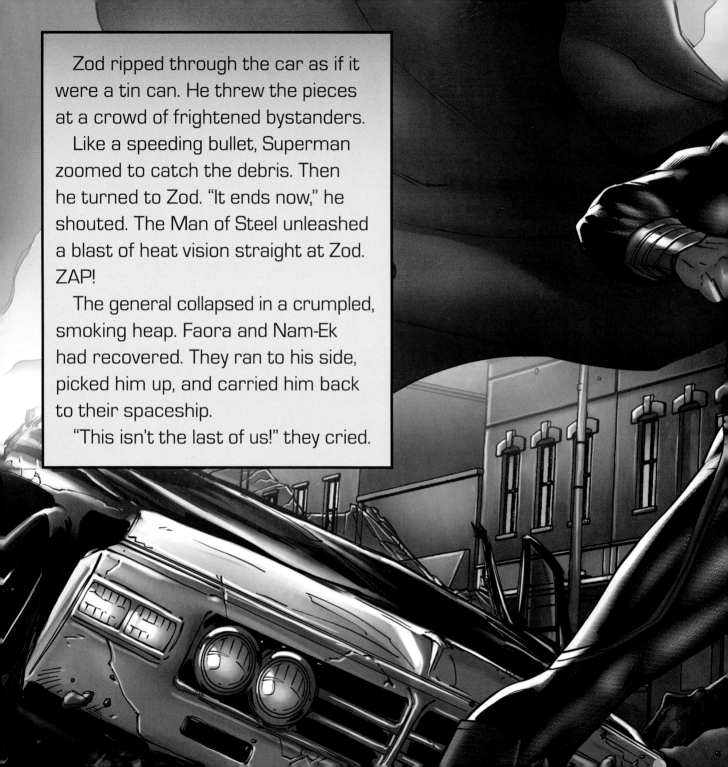

Zod ripped through the car as if it were a tin can. He threw the pieces at a crowd of frightened bystanders.

Like a speeding bullet, Superman zoomed to catch the debris. Then he turned to Zod. "It ends now," he shouted. The Man of Steel unleashed a blast of heat vision straight at Zod. ZAP!

The general collapsed in a crumpled, smoking heap. Faora and Nam-Ek had recovered. They ran to his side, picked him up, and carried him back to their spaceship.

"This isn't the last of us!" they cried.

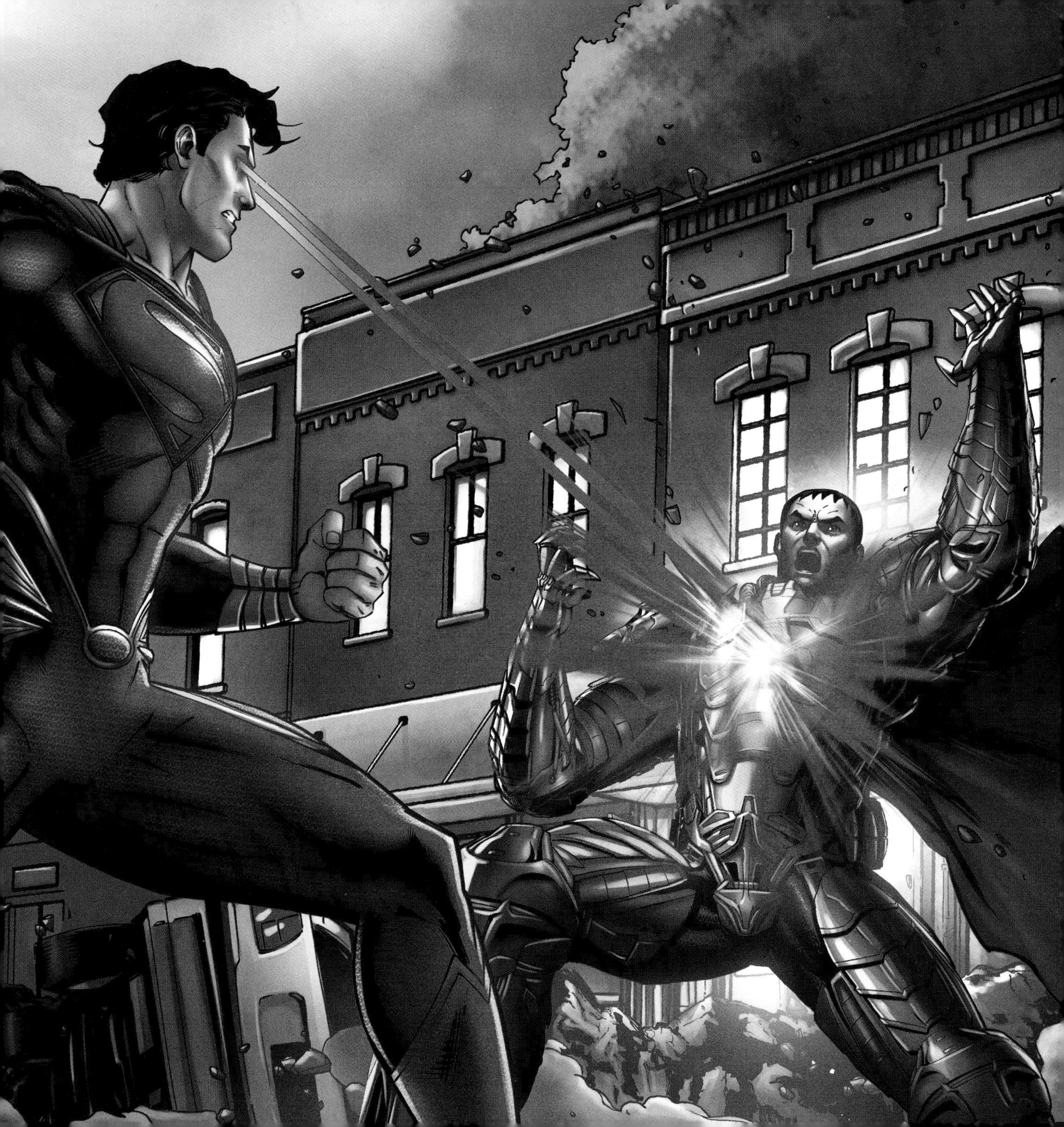

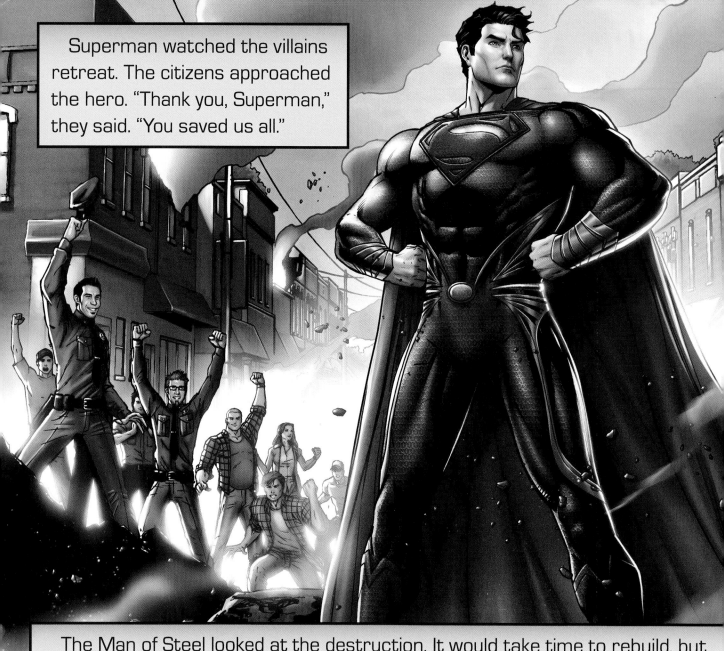

Superman watched the villains retreat. The citizens approached the hero. "Thank you, Superman," they said. "You saved us all."

The Man of Steel looked at the destruction. It would take time to rebuild, but Superman knew that the people of his new world were resilient and strong. He had learned so much on Earth, and he was very proud to call it home.